HOPSCOTCH
ADVENTURES

Sinbad
and the
Diamond Valley

by Martin Waddell and O'Kif

W

FRANKLIN WA

LONDON • SYDNE

First published in 2009 by
Franklin Watts
338 Euston Road
London
NW1 3BH

Franklin Watts Australia
Level 17/207 Kent Street
Sydney
NSW 2000

Text © Martin Waddell 2009
Illustrations © O'Kif 2009

The rights of Martin Waddell to be identified as the author
and O'Kif as the illustrator of this Work have been asserted
in accordance with the Copyright, Designs and Patents Act, 1988.

A CIP catalogue record for this book is available
from the British Library.

ISBN 978 0 7496 8554 6 (hbk)
ISBN 978 0 7496 8566 9 (pbk)

Series Editor: Jackie Hamley
Series Advisor: Dr Barrie Wade
Series Designer: Peter Scoulding

Printed in China

Franklin Watts is a division of
Hachette Children's Books,
an Hachette UK company
www.hachette.co.uk

Sinbad the Sailor was shipwrecked
on an island with his friend Ali.

They stood on top of a cliff
looking down on a valley
littered with rocks.

In the sunlight, the rocks down below sparkled as though the valley was covered in precious jewels.

"Diamonds!" cried Ali.

"Let's climb down and check,"
said Sinbad.

"It's a valley of diamonds!"
shouted Ali. "We're rich!"

They both filled their pockets with
diamonds, and soon they had all
they could carry.

But beady eyes were watching.
THINGS came from the rocks,
slithering towards them unseen.

"Snakes!" Ali yelled. "It's a valley of diamonds and snakes!" There were snakes all around Sinbad and Ali.

"Run Ali!" cried Sinbad.
They ran through the rocks as
they tried to escape from the
snakes and then...

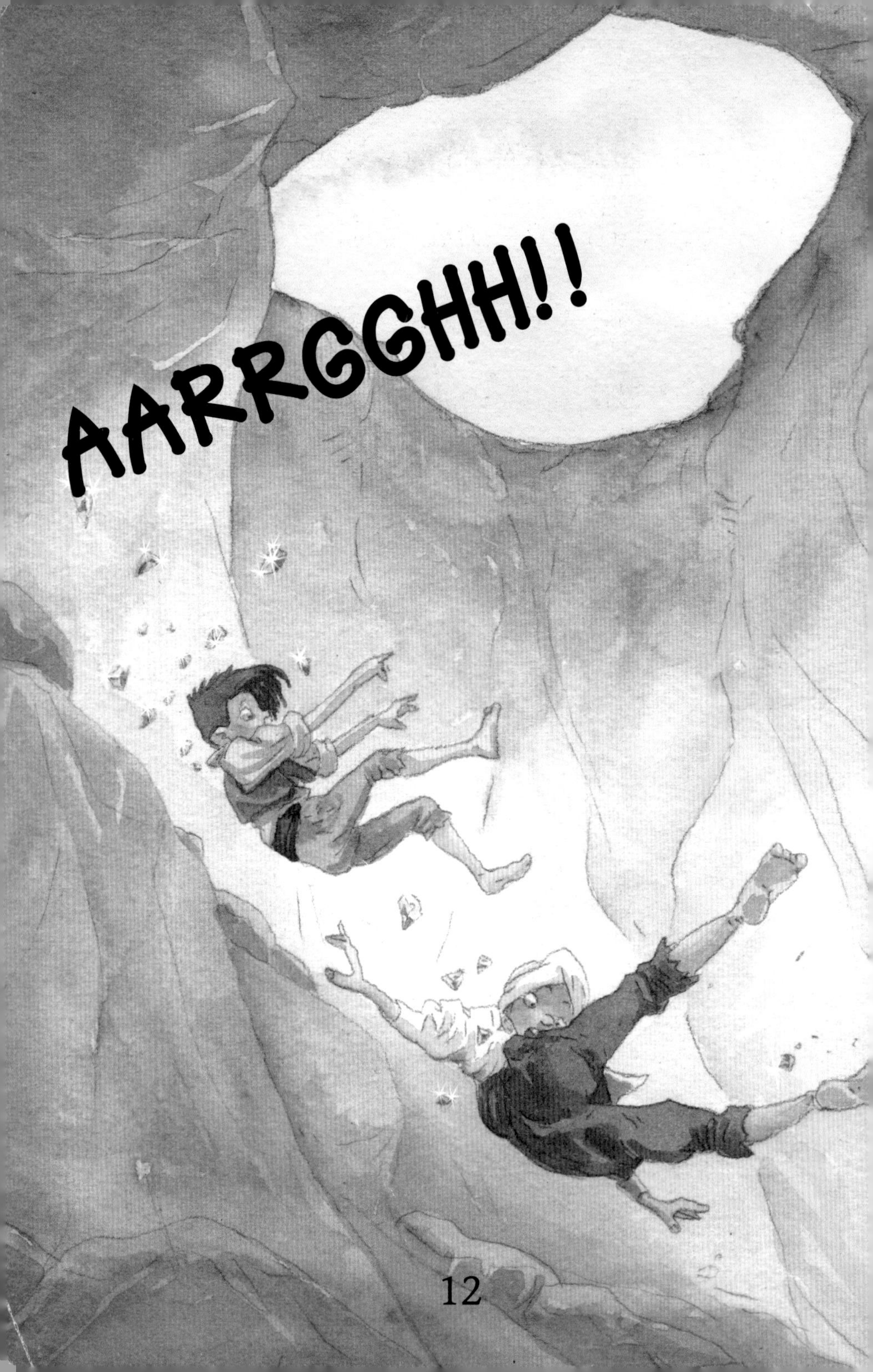
AARRGGHH!!

Ali screamed as they
stumbled and fell...
down, down, down
through a gap
in the rocks.

PLOP! They landed on a soft tangle of feathers beside something very large and white.

"Is that a bird's egg?" Ali panted.
"It is, and we're in a bird's nest,"
frowned Sinbad.

"It must be a big bird to lay a
huge egg like that," gasped Ali.
"Don't look behind you,"
said Sinbad. "It is!"

They hid in the bird's nest as the bird ate the snake it had caught.

"That bird looks hungry to me!"
groaned Ali. "How do we get
out of this?"

"Think, think, THINK!" Sinbad said. And he thought...

And he thought...

20

"We hitch a lift!" Sinbad grinned.
"When the bird flies, we fly!"

Next time the bird flew, they flew too, hanging onto its legs, but...

...the bird dived to attack a sea serpent. Sinbad and Ali were back at sea!

"Think Sinbad!" choked Ali, as the waves broke over his head. "These diamonds are heavy and I'm sinking fast."

"We don't think this time," Sinbad
laughed. "We stand up and paddle."

"Paddle where?" gasped Ali.

"Just follow me," said Sinbad.

When they reached dry land they sold the diamonds they had left...

...though Sinbad kept one for Mrs Sinbad, and Ali kept one for his mum!

Puzzle 1

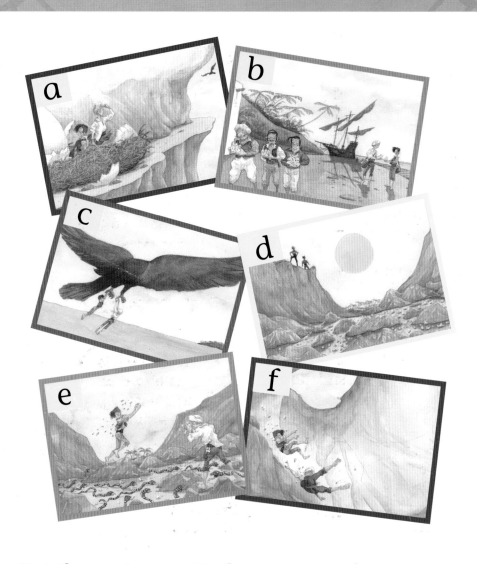

Put these pictures in the correct order.
Which event do you think is most important?
Now try writing the story in your own words!

Choose the correct speech bubbles for the characters above. Can you think of any others? Turn over to find the answers.

Answers

Puzzle 1

The correct order is: 1d, 2e, 3f, 4a, 5c, 6b

Puzzle 2

Sinbad: 2, 5, 6

Ali: 1, 3, 4

Look out for more Hopscotch Adventures:

TALES OF KING ARTHUR

1. The Sword in the Stone
ISBN 978 0 7496 6694 1

2. Arthur the King
ISBN 978 0 7496 6695 8

3. The Round Table
ISBN 978 0 7496 6697 2

4. Sir Lancelot and the Ice Castle
ISBN 978 0 7496 6698 9

5. Sir Gawain and the Green Knight
ISBN 978 0 7496 8557 7*
ISBN 978 0 7496 8569 0

6. Sir Galahad and the Holy Grail
ISBN 978 0 7496 8558 4*
ISBN 978 0 7496 8570 6

TALES OF ROBIN HOOD

Robin and the Knight
ISBN 978 0 7496 6699 6

Robin and the Monk
ISBN 978 0 7496 6700 9

Robin and the Silver Arrow
ISBN 978 0 7496 6703 0

Robin and the Friar
ISBN 978 0 7496 6702 3

Robin and the Butcher
ISBN 978 0 7496 8555 3*
ISBN 978 0 7496 8568 3

Robin and Maid Marian
ISBN 978 0 7496 8556 0*
ISBN 978 0 7496 8567 6

TALES OF SINBAD THE SAILOR

Sinbad and the Ogre
ISBN 978 0 7496 8559 1*
ISBN 978 0 7496 8571 3

Sinbad and the Whale
ISBN 978 0 7496 8553 9*
ISBN 978 0 7496 8565 2

Sinbad and the Diamond Valley
ISBN 978 0 7496 8554 6*
ISBN 978 0 7496 8566 9

Sinbad and the Monkeys
ISBN 978 0 7496 8560 7*
ISBN 978 0 7496 8572 0

For more *Hopscotch Adventures* and other *Hopscotch* stories,
visit:
www.franklinwatts.co.uk

* hardback